This book belongs
to
THE VINEYARD SCHOOL

RUTH BROWN'S

Mad Summer Night's Dream

for Colin and Hilary

A Red Fox Book

Published by Random House Children's Books
20 Vauxhall Bridge Road, London SW1V 2SA
A division of The Random House Group Ltd
London Melbourne Sydney Auckland
Johannesburg and agencies throughout the world

Copyright © Ruth Brown 1998

1 3 5 7 9 10 8 6 4 2

First published in Great Britain by Andersen Press Ltd 1998

Red Fox edition 2000

Printed and bound in Hong Kong

THE RANDOM HOUSE GROUP Limited Reg. No. 954009
www.randomhouse.co.uk

ISBN 0 09 940296 3

Ruth Brown's
Mad Summer Night's Dream

Written and Illustrated by Ruth Brown

RED FOX

It was midsummer night in winter
and snow was on the ground,

When miles away, inside my head,
I heard an eerie sound.

I went down to the cellar
to look from an upstairs room,

The flowers were singing sweetly,
the birds were in full bloom.

Quite clearly in the distance,
but almost out of sight,

two fat cats were yowling,
preparing for a fight.

They were staring at each other
while sitting back to back.
One was black with brown stripes,
the brown one's stripes were black.

Three stone monkeys sprang to life,
and danced around with glee.
The blind one said, "I volunteer
to be the referee."
He said he'd watch the hissing cats
to supervise fair play —
The silent monkey by his side
said, "That will be the day!"
The other monkey next to him
said he would keep the score,
for though he couldn't hear a thing,
he'd heard it all before.

But as they started fighting
the wall came tumbling down;

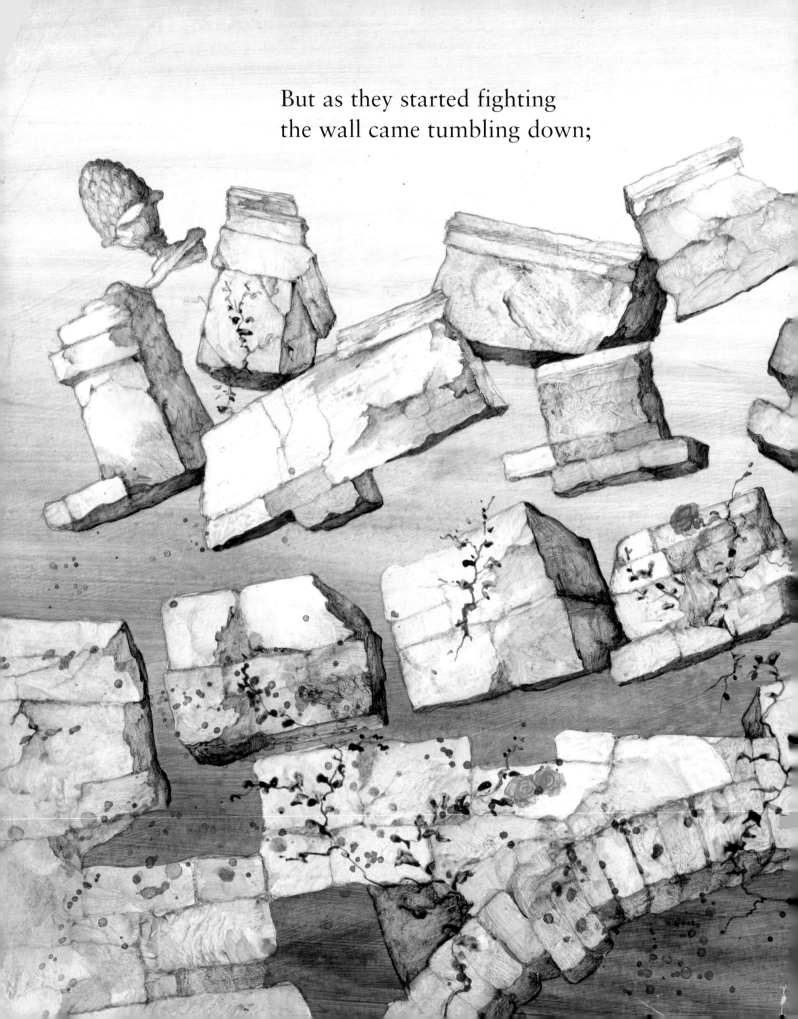

The cats fell into a dried-up ditch —
I thought that they would drown.

I jumped straight in to save them,
and heard a piercing scream...

It woke me up —

— it was morning!
What a mad midsummer night's dream.

Some bestselling Red Fox picture books